| | |

Summer Camp is published by Stone Arch Books,
A Capstone Imprint
1710 Roe Crest Drive
North Mankato, Minnesota 56003

Copyright © 2017 Stone Arch Books

Library of Congress Cataloging-in-Publication Data
Names: Brandes, Wendy L., 1965- author. | Lorenzet, Eleonora,
   illustrator.
Title: Emily's pranking problem / by Wendy L. Brandes ;
   [illustrator, Eleonora Lorenzet].
Description: North Mankato, Minnesota : Stone Arch Books, an imprint
   of Capstone Press, [2017] | Series: Summer camp | Summary:
   Twelve-year-old Emily wants to enjoy summer camp, with its
   competitions and pranks and just not think about the possibility that
   her parents may be breaking up—but the stress of keeping that
   problem secret is giving her pranks an edge that sometimes makes
   them a little less than funny, and even a little mean.
Identifiers: LCCN 2016020951 | ISBN 9781496525994 (library binding)
   | ISBN 9781496527127 (pbk.) | ISBN 9781496527165 (ebook pdf)
Subjects: LCSH: Children of separated parents—Juvenile fiction. |
   Practical jokes—Juvenile fiction. | Camps—Juvenile fiction. | Stress
   (Psychology)—Juvenile fiction. | Friendship—Juvenile fiction. |
   CYAC: Practical jokes—Fiction. | Divorce—Fiction. | Camps—
   Fiction. | Stress (Psychology—Fiction. | Friendship—Fiction.
Classification: LCC PZ7.1.B7515 Em 2017 | DDC 813.6 [Fic]—dc23
LC record available at https://lccn.loc.gov/2016020951

Illustrated by Eleonora Lorenzet

Printed and bound in the USA
009661CGF16

| | |

≫—— SUMMER CAMP →

EMILY'S PRANKING PROBLEM

BY WENDY L. BRANDES

STONE ARCH BOOKS
a capstone imprint

FIND YOUR ADVENTURE AT

CAMP MON MON LAKE!

Camp Mon Mon Lake, an all-girls sleepaway camp in Maine, has it all! Girls return year after year for friendship, challenges, and fun. And every year, they take home memories of a magical summer filled with the warmth of a summer family.

We group our campers according to age. Each group is assigned a different bird name—and there are A LOT of different birds up here! Our youngest group is the Hummingbirds (ages 7–8) and our oldest group is the Condors, also known as the Seniors (ages 14–15). In between we have Blue Jays, Robins, and Songbirds.

At Mon Mon Lake, we fill the weeks with singing, spirit, activity, and group bonding. No matter what your interests are, we have an activity for you!

MON MON'S SUMMER ACTIVITIES

LAND SPORTS

ARCHERY
BASKETBALL
CLIMBING WALL
FIELD HOCKEY
GYMNASTICS
LACROSSE
RIDING
SOCCER
SOFTBALL
TENNIS
VOLLEYBALL
YOGA

WATER SPORTS

CANOEING
KAYAKING
SAILING
SWIMMING
WATERSKIING

THE ARTS

DANCE
DRAMA
DRAWING
PAINTING
POTTERY

WHAT CAMPERS ARE SAYING:

"I didn't want to come to camp at all, but that's before I met my bunkmates. The girls at Camp Mon Mon make the best friends."
— MJ, a new camper

"I love the swimming, the intercamp games, and all the fun in the bunk—especially pranking our counselors!"
— Emily, a four-year camp veteran

"I love the group shows. Being onstage in front of the entire camp—and the boys' camp next door—is amazing! No place is more fun than Camp Mon Mon Lake!"
— Nina, a Blue Jay (age 13)

"The camp trips are my favorite part about camp. What could be better than hiking and camping out with your best friends?"
— Claire, award winner for Best Outdoorswoman

CHAPTER 1

We were two weeks into my fifth year at Camp Mon Mon Lake. Some of the best parts of summer were still ahead—Color War, the hiking and canoeing trip, the Tri-Camp Games, the Group Show, and Brother-Sister Day with Eagle Rock, the boys' camp. Being the super-competitive twelve-year-old girl that I am, I loved it all. And I think I loved it more than ever this year, because it meant I wouldn't be at home.

My parents had been fighting a lot during the past few months—huge blowouts over really stupid things. Maybe Dad would lose his keys and he would start grumbling. Then within a few minutes, he and Mom would be screaming at each other. Or Mom would get totally angry if Dad was running late, and she'd completely lose her cool. The whole year was like that.

So my older brother, Zac, and I were more excited than usual to go to camp—just to get away from everything at home. We counted down the days till our buses left.

Even though I usually jump right in and share my every thought about everything, I didn't want anyone at camp to know about what was going on at home. I wanted everyone to think I was the same Emily that I'd always been. I worried that if they knew, they'd treat me differently. And then there would be endless questions about whether I'm okay.

Instead, I wanted to talk about swimming times, Backward Day, campfires, and especially, pranking my counselor. I love to test the rules. That's what makes camp so much fun.

"Susannah has been a total buzzkill for the past two weeks. Since when do counselors make the twelve- and thirteen-year-olds stay in the bunk for rest?" I asked my bunkmates during our mandatory rest hour. In my bunk were Nina and Claire, who I had been with for the past four years, and Zoe and MJ, who were new.

We all got along great, and our only big issue had been an argument between MJ and Zoe. See, Zoe's dad is a super-famous rock star, and she didn't want anyone at camp to know. MJ figured it out and wrote home about it, and when Zoe found out, she got mad. But being the total loudmouth that I am, I helped fix it all by telling Zoe that everyone knew her dad was famous and it wasn't a big deal.

"Susannah's only following the rules," Claire said. Was she actually defending our counselor?

"That's the point, Goody Two-shoes," I said. "She's treating us like we're babies. The other Blue Jay bunks don't have to stay in for an hour during rest time."

"True," Nina responded. "They go wherever they want after lunch."

"Plus, when MJ got that package that had gum balls in it, Susannah took them," I complained.

"That *was* pretty obnoxious," MJ said. "I mean, it was only gum. Even Aunt Alice doesn't have a problem with gum, and she's the one who makes the rules."

"Exactly! It's time for action!" I exclaimed.

"Uh-oh," Nina said. "You mean it's time to get into trouble?"

I laughed. "If that's what it takes!"

"Can't we just talk to Aunt Alice about it?" Zoe asked.

"Do you really think the head of the camp is going to side with us because the counselor is following *her* rules too strictly?" I asked.

"Okay, so what are you thinking?" Claire asked.

"A prank. Something simple, but funny." I smirked.

"Won't Susannah just go crazy if we prank her?" Nina asked.

"You guys don't think she has any sense of humor?" I replied.

Practically in unison, everyone screamed, "No!" We all cracked up.

"So, you do realize that pranking her isn't going to get anyone to think we deserve to have free time during rest," Nina said seriously.

"I know, but at least it'll be fun! Like camp's supposed to be!" I said. "Remember last year? When we put makeup on all the other Sparrows' faces while they slept. That was *awe-some!*"

"Sounds funny! Did they take it well?" Zoe asked.

"Yeah, but then they got us back by hiding all of our bunk's toilet paper," Claire replied.

MJ and Zoe giggled. "So what happened?"

"Well, I got stranded in the stall," Nina complained. "I had to wait until someone came back from breakfast, and I could yell for them. That's why *I'm* the one who's worried about another prank!"

"Blah, blah, blah. No toilet paper. You were alone in the stall for what, five minutes?" I answered.

"It felt like an hour. And I missed half of my scheduled ropes course," Nina said, pouting.

Zoe and MJ laughed again. Then Zoe said, "Sorry, Nina. That doesn't sound too fun. But you've got to admit, it's kind of funny."

"Ha, ha," Nina said dryly.

"Okay, so moving on from last year, is everyone up for pranking Susannah?" I asked.

"Maybe . . . What if we asked Astrid to help," MJ said, referring to our other counselor, who came all the way from Sweden.

"You're such a newbie. It's so cute!" I replied. "Astrid is cool. And probably, if she were a camper, she'd be in. But counselors have a code. Unless it's something that the camp says is okay, she won't help us."

"Susannah wouldn't get too mad if we short-sheeted her bed, right?" MJ said.

"Too tame," I replied.

"Tame won't get us into trouble, though," Nina said.

"Dye in her toothpaste?" I asked.

"Too mean," Zoe said. "What about itching powder?"

"You just said that dye in her toothpaste was too mean. Itching powder is like a million times worse," Claire replied.

"Substitute salt for sugar? Or sugar for salt in the dining hall?" Zoe asked.

"Not bad," I said.

"What about the one where you change her clothes with someone's who's smaller? Then she'd think she gained weight. After that, we could substitute clothes from someone who's bigger," Nina said, finally getting into the spirit of it.

"That could be fun," I said. "But then we'd need to get other counselors' clothes. And, like I said, they won't help. What about sending her shoes off in a canoe?"

"All of them?" MJ asked.

I shrugged. "Some? All? One pair? I don't know. Or we could put leaves in her bed and pretend they're poison ivy."

"Mean," Claire said.

"How about a water balloon under her pillow?" I asked, thinking quickly.

"*Ooooooh,*" MJ said. "That's a great one."

"She will be *soooo* mad!" Nina said excitedly.

"Is everyone in?" I asked. Everyone nodded.

"Game on! We'll make a plan!" I said, happy we agreed on something. Even if it was a teensy bit lame . . .

CHAPTER 2

The next morning, three of the Condors—the senior group—burst into our bunk, walking backward and wearing their clothes inside out. *"Draw k-cab yad, draw k-cab yad!"* they yelled. *"Rennid emit! Rennid emit!"*

Backward Day! One of my favorites of the whole summer. Starting with *rennid* (dinner), we went through the whole day backward: dinner, a show starring the boy counselors, afternoon activities, lunch, morning activities, flag raising, breakfast, and then sleep. Walking backward was optional.

"*Teg pu, teg pu*!" I screamed to my bunkmates, wondering if MJ and Zoe would have any idea what this was all about and that *teg pu* meant *get up* on Backward Day!

I put my clothes on backward and went to find my camp sister, eight-year-old Julia. Older camp sisters were assigned to the younger girls to show them the ropes.

I knew Julia would be confused about Backward Day, so I barged into her bunk. She was sitting on her bed, unsure about whether she had to try to put her shoes and swimsuit on backward.

"Okay, *Luj*, let's start with your shoes. Put them on regular or your feet are going to hurt!"

I tickled her and she collapsed on her bed screaming, "Stop, stop, stop!"

"It's Backward Day, *Luj*. What do you have to say?" I teased.

She kept laughing and said, "Please?"

"Think hard! Backward Day!"

"Pots! Pots! Pots!" she yelled.

"Good!" I pulled her to her feet. "You wear your swimsuit forward, and you can swim the backstroke."

"I'm not so good at swimming backstroke though. Could I do sidestroke?" she asked seriously.

Was I that serious when I was her age? No way. Always a rule breaker—at least a little bit—even when I was a squirt. "Whatever you do is going to be fine. Just have fun! Now come with me for *rennid*!"

I held her hand and walked her backward out of her bunk. We saw lots of other campers walking backward to the dining hall, while Angus, the Australian head swim counselor, walked on his hands!

For meals this week, we were seated by first name— the four other Emilys were at my table, along with two Emmas and an Ella. It made meals confusing but fun. At our table, we renamed ourselves according

to our favorite activity at camp, just in case you needed to get someone's attention to pass the bread or something.

Emily A.C. (arts and crafts) was sitting next to me on one side and Emily-Tennis was on my other. Today it was dessert first—chocolate cake and ice cream in the morning. The absolute best. The problem with *rennid*, though, was always the main course. Too heavy for eight in the morning. This year it was pasta with red sauce. Just seeing the cheese shaker in the center of the table made me feel a little bit sick.

Looking around, I saw Julia—with the eight other camp Julias—totally smeared with spaghetti sauce. Funny! Then I saw Susannah, who was sitting at the Anne/Anna/Ana/Suzy table. She gave me a big smile, like she thought Backward Day was cool. I started feeling bad that I had been annoyed with her. Holding off the prank might be a good idea.

Emily A.C., who is in the Songbirds, the group ahead of mine, asked if my brother, Zac, was coming for sibs day over the weekend.

"Um-hum," I said, mouth completely full of pasta. "Do you have a brother at Eagle Rock?"

"No, he used to go there, but he's too old for camp now. Anyway, he stopped before he was an Oak because he wanted to swim more seriously," she said.

"I love swimming! You know that my name is Emily Swimily for a reason! What are his times?" I asked. "I've thought of taking a summer off and just swimming, but I'd miss camp way too much!"

"You know, Mac was thinking of doing that too," Emily A.C. said.

Ugh. MacKenzie Sciappi, former bunkmate and general nuisance. There was no way she was *really* thinking about swimming competitively. She probably just said that to make everyone think she was better than she was. "Oh, really? I didn't realize that Mac took it that seriously."

"Are you guys talking about Mac?" Emily-Tennis chimed in. "She was telling me that she might swim anchor in the Tri-Camp relay this year."

I nearly choked on my garlic bread. I'd *always* been the anchor for the relay team. Mac knew that. Why would she be telling everyone that she would be swimming that leg this year?

I looked over at her table, and she winked at me. Seriously? What kid our age winks? Sometimes it was like she was a forty-year-old in a kid's body, totally disapproving of anything fun. When she was my bunkmate, she tattled on me more than a few times too. And other times, she just was so braggy, like she was the best at everything. Still, people *actually* liked her. I sometimes wondered whether I was missing something, or they were.

"Well, she must have gotten *much* better at swimming then," I said. As it came out of my mouth, I realized how snotty it sounded. It *was* true, though.

"Ouch, that's harsh," Emily-Tennis said.

"You know what I mean," I said, smiling and trying to shrug it off.

"What's the Blue Jays' bunk show going to be, Swimily?" she asked, changing the subject.

"Oh, I think it's *Wicked*, but that's not my thing at all," I said. "I'm usually in the back holding up scenery or something."

"You've definitely got the personality to be onstage, though," Yoga Emma said.

"*Hmmmm*. Is that cause I'm loud and pushy?" I asked, laughing. All the Emilys, Emmas, and the one Ella laughed along too.

We finished our backward *rennid* by putting napkins on our laps and singing a dinner song.

Next up was the boy counselor show. We had all acted like it was night and brought our flashlights just for fun. Then it was shower hour—at ten in the morning!—followed by regular activities. It didn't make sense to shower *before* jumping in the lake, but that's how Backward Day worked.

I walked backward down to the waterfront for afternoon swim (in the morning). Because I was a competitive swimmer, Angus and the waterfront staff just let me get my laps in, rather than making me take lessons. Best of all, sometimes Angus would time me.

"Miss Emily, so good of you to come," Angus said with a salute.

I tried my best Australian accent. "G'day, Angus."

"You ready for some hard *yakka*?" he asked.

"What does that even mean?" I wondered.

"Hard work, Emily. Hard work. Time to dive in. Swim a few to get warmed up, and then I'll time you."

I did as I was told. I jumped in and did five freestyle laps, five breaststrokes, one butterfly (it's so hard to get your arms flying over your head first thing in the morning), and two backstrokes. Within ten minutes, Angus had me racing from side to side, trying to beat my best Mon Mon time from this year in the 100-meter freestyle.

Totally exhausted after my last try, I hit the wall and then floated in my lane, catching my breath.

"Em! You just shaved one half second off your best time! Well done!" Angus shouted.

"Let me see the stopwatch!" I yelled. Hearing that I beat my time gave me a burst of energy. I hopped out of the lane and onto the dock.

"Yay!" I screamed. "One half second is huge! Especially in a lake full of seaweed and fish!"

"It *is* great! Next time, I'm going to get the fish to chase you to make you go even faster!" Angus said. I laughed.

"Your parents will be so excited to see you swim on visiting day. I loved it last year when your mom jumped in after you broke your best time in breaststroke."

My parents . . . the last thing I wanted to think about. It was Backward Day, though, so maybe hearing about my parents being happy and having fun last year was okay. Because it was definitely backward from how they were now.

CHAPTER 3

All of the stuff about my parents floated in my head as I walked back from swim. It was the first time I'd really wanted to cry since I got to camp. And to make things worse, I ran right into MacKenzie, who I knew was going to get under my skin. Great.

"Hi, Mac," I said, with zero enthusiasm.

"Hey, Emily. How was your time? I saw Angus was clocking you."

"Yeah. I shaved a half second off my best."

"Half second, huh? I'm a full second down from last year," Mac replied.

No matter what I said, she always had to top me.

"Oh, that's great," I said, thinking what a pain in the neck she was.

"I heard that you didn't think I was good enough to swim anchor for the Tri-Camp Games," she said.

I laughed. "Only after I heard that you'd said that you were going to replace me."

"Oh, right, *you* usually swim anchor," she said, as if she had actually forgotten.

"Well, I swam anchor when we won the relay last year," I said. *After you blew a fifteen-meter lead*, I added to myself. "Maybe we can win it again this year."

"Well, no matter who swims anchor, it's always fun being on the relay team with you, Emily," she said, smiling a huge grin.

Was she being serious? Or was she being sarcastic again? I hated it when she was sort of nice. I never knew whether I could trust her or not.

"Anyway, we have Brother-Sister Day before Tri-Camps. That's what I'm looking forward to," I said.

"Oh, right. So Zac is coming here this weekend? He's *sooooo* cute," she said.

And she was *sooooo* annoying.

Two days later, Zac hopped off the Eagle Rock van along with Owen, his best friend from camp. Owen's sister, Maggie, is a Robin, two years younger than me. Brother-Sister Day is a big deal here. And there were two of them to look forward to: brothers from Eagle Rock came to Mon Mon on a weekend early in the summer, and then all the sisters went to Eagle Rock right before the summer ended.

Zac spotted me, jogged over, and gave me a hug. Owen was right behind him. From Owen I got a, "*Wasssupp*, Em? How's my favorite Mon Mon camper, besides my sister, of course?"

"As fabulous as ever," I replied.

"Show me your bunk for this year," Zac said.

We walked over to 12A, and I knocked on the door, yelling, "Incoming boy. Boy incoming."

Nina, MJ, and Zoe were hanging out. I was glad that Susannah wasn't there because she probably would have found some rule in the handbook that said brothers couldn't come in.

"Hey, Bunk 12!" Zac shouted.

"Don't forget the A!" Zoe said, smiling.

"Zac, this is Zoe. She's from England and her father's famous."

"Thanks so much, Emily. You know I totally love it when you tell people that," Zoe said sarcastically.

"Just wanted to get it out of the way," I said.

"Nice to meet you, famous Zoe," Zac said.

"You too," Zoe said.

"Do you speak British?" Zac asked.

Zoe giggled. "Did you have your porridge this morning? Are you knackered after your trip from Eagle Rock? Need to use the loo?"

Zac laughed. "That's great!"

"And this is MJ. No famous people in her family. She's a huge Yankees fan though," I said. "And you know Nina from many years of camp."

Zac plopped on my bed. "So what's going on at Mon Mon? You have a Tri-Camp race coming up?" he asked.

"Next week," I said.

"And you have a totally annoying counselor?"

"Shush! She lurks around," I replied.

He lowered his voice. "If I know you, you're planning a prank. Itching powder? Hot sauce in her ketchup bottle?"

"You guys are much meaner than we are," I said. "Something tame."

"Any suggestions?" Nina asked. "We have a plan, but maybe you'll come up with something better."

"Ideas for pranks? You could hide all of her underwear," Zac said.

Everyone laughed. "Maybe—" Nina's thought was interrupted by the door jingling and a small "hello."

"Hi, guys. Owen wanted to see what you were up to," Maggie said, dragging her brother in by the hand.

"Owen, this is the ever-fabulous Bunk 12A. Everyone, this is Owen," I said.

After everyone introduced themselves, Owen asked, "What are you guys planning to do today?"

"Wanna go tubing? You think they'd let us?" Zac asked. "We're allowed at Eagle Rock."

"Would they let me tube even if I haven't passed my level-four swim test?" Maggie asked.

"Let's find out," I said.

In a nanosecond, the four of us were out the door. When we got down to the waterfront, we ran right into Mac.

"Hey, Emily. Hi, Mags!" she said cheerfully. "Oh, hey, Zac. Remember me from last year?"

Vomit. Mac was actually flirting with my brother. Totally uncool. Was it her *project* to totally get in my face this summer?

"Oh yeah. You were in my sister's bunk. MacDonough, right?" Zac asked.

"MacKenzie. But everyone calls me Mac."

"Hi, Mac. I'm Owen."

She'd better not flirt with Owen too. "Mags told me about you, Owen," she said, smiling.

Barf a second time. I guess Maggie didn't like it either, because she hurried us along. "C'mon, guys," Maggie said. "We have to see if we can tube together."

"I *loooove* tubing," Mac said, waiting for us to invite her. "I'm a really good spotter when I'm on the boat—"

"Oh, we could use a good spotter," Zac said.

"Then I'll come with you!" Mac exclaimed.

Argh. I wanted to strangle her—we were going to be stuck with her on a boat as she talked in a fake singsong voice to both boys. She was so, so annoying.

After an afternoon of tubing, we were finally able to ditch Mac. Zac and I walked to the Don, Camp Mon Mon's rec center, before the boys headed back to Eagle Rock. We had the place to ourselves.

"Have you heard anything from Mom?" I asked. I knew that it might end our day in an unhappy way, but I had to ask.

"She wrote that she was staying with Aunt Steph this week," Zac said.

"Yeah, she told me the same thing," I replied.

"I also got a weird email from Dad, saying he was going to visit his college friend Carl Lee up in Bridgeton. He said he might come to visit me a day before visiting day because he'll already be in the area," Zac said.

"Does that mean they won't be coming up here together?" I paused. "Are they done with each other?" I felt my eyes start to fill up.

"Don't cry, Em. We don't know what's happening."

I wiped my tears.

Zac continued, "We'll get through all of this. Maybe it's better if they're not together. All the fighting is killer."

I wiped my eyes again. "I know, I know. It's just so weird, you know? I'm glad we're up here, where everything's the same and there's no yelling. But then I worry about what it's going to be like when we go home."

"We'll figure that out when it happens. In the meantime, we just have to have fun while we're here. C'mon," he said, pulling on my arm. "I wanna see if you can do a cartwheel."

I laughed. At home Zac made this rule that we could only talk about what was going on with our parents for ten minutes at a time. He thought that we shouldn't get too stuck in their problems, so ten minutes was enough. "Are you saying that we've hit our ten-minute limit?"

He smiled. "Cartwheel, please."

I've been trying to do a perfect cartwheel since I was a seven-year-old Hummingbird. Back when our parents didn't totally hate each other. "I'm still terrible, but I'll show you," I said.

We went outside, and I did my best impression of someone doing a cartwheel. Zac laughed and applauded as I tilted way to the left but ended up on my feet.

CHAPTER 4

After talking about Mom and Dad with Zac, I just wanted to stop thinking about home and throw myself into something fun. And prank-planning was definitely the answer.

"Bunk meeting!" I shouted when I got back to the bunk after saying goodbye to Zac. We all gathered on Claire's bed. "We need a prank."

"Don't we have one? Susannah and the water-balloon prank?" Claire said.

"Yeah, but we checked out MJ's balloons, and they're regular ones," I explained. "We'll have to wait for her mom to send her some water ones. In the meantime, let's do something else. Something funny."

"Maybe we could prank Astrid," MJ suggested.

"She'd totally be a good sport about it," Nina replied.

"Oh, and maybe it would inspire Susannah to be a good sport when the water balloons finally arrive!" Zoe added.

"Could we do some sort of joke involving Lars?" Claire asked. Lars was Astrid's best friend from home who came to camp with her. We constantly teased her about crushing on him.

"She'd murder us," I said. "What about something to do with all the fish she eats."

"No. No. No. Her breakfast! You know how she eats that hot oatmeal every morning," MJ exclaimed.

"Hey, what if we made her breakfast super-hot?" I said, smiling.

Zoe giggled. "What're you thinking?"

"Spice up her cereal!" I said. "I know we have some cinnamon candy hidden somewhere in the bunk!"

After taps that night, we checked out our secret stash of candy. It was hidden in Mr. Snuggles, a bear that I had brought from home. Nina spilled the candy out onto my bed, and after we ate through some gummy bears and licorice bits, we found the perfect ingredient for Astrid's oatmeal prank: Super Nova Eights—the hottest candy around. We'd give a great cinnamony start to Astrid's morning!

We poured about twenty candies out of the box and hid them in an envelope. Prank on!

The next morning, we were back to sitting with our bunkmates for breakfast. MJ and I made sure to sit next to Astrid. MJ had ten Super Novas and I had the rest. As soon as Astrid sat down with her cereal, Nina came and asked if she could speak to Astrid privately. Nina was going to make up something about having lost a retainer and needing to see the orthodontist.

When Astrid walked away, MJ dumped her stash of cinnamon candy into the bowl. They sat there like red pebbles on top of the oatmeal. Not what we expected. I mixed them around, but they weren't melting quickly like we thought they would.

"What do we do?" MJ whispered.

I replied, "Hmm, try hiding them at the bottom maybe." I dumped mine in, and they seemed to melt a little faster, slowly disappearing, leaving a blood red trail behind.

MJ looked toward the entrance of the dining hall. "Nina's still got Astrid tied up," she said.

I signaled Nina to keep stalling, while MJ mixed the Super Novas in, stirring faster and faster.

"What if Astrid cracks her teeth? Or chokes? Maybe we should give it up," MJ said, slightly panicked.

"No, we'll be good," I said. I took the spoon and went digging toward the bottom of the bowl to see if any of the pieces were still like stones. They had melted, but the oatmeal had started to look very pinkish.

Meanwhile, Nina looked like she was crying—an excellent distraction.

"What are you doing to Astrid's food?" asked one of the senior Condor girls at our table.

"Trying to keep it warm for her," I said, thinking fast.

"You know that stirring it makes it get cold quicker," she said in a kind of senior, know-it-all way.

"Oh, I didn't realize that," I said, dropping the spoon. "You mean we might have made it colder by accident?"

"No biggie. I'm sure it's still hot," she said.

"I'm sure too," I said, knowing that it would definitely be "hot" when she ate it!

Astrid came back to the table and sat down. MJ and I tried to keep her from getting a glimpse before she started eating the now strangely pink cereal in front of her. Meanwhile, Zoe, Claire, and Nina were all staring at Astrid, waiting for her reaction.

She was about to take a mouthful, but then put her spoon back in the bowl and got up. "Don't clear my plate," she called. "I just have to tell Rachel that Nina may need to go to the orthodontist." Rachel Richardson was the head counselor, in charge of our Blue Jay group. R^2, as we called her, would have to okay a trip to the orthodontist—if Nina actually needed one, that is.

"Okay," I said slowly, wishing she had taken a bite. But on the bright side, maybe this meant that she was going to eat more quickly and wouldn't notice the color.

"What do we do?" MJ whispered.

I shrugged. "We'll see what happens."

Astrid came back, sat down, picked up her spoon, and took her first bite. She didn't seem to see the pinkness. And she immediately started fanning her mouth.

"Why does this taste so hot!" she exclaimed, mouth full of oatmeal.

She grabbed for her water glass, downed the whole thing, and started fanning her mouth again. All of us 12A girls started giggling.

"Have I been punked?" she asked.

We laughed even harder.

She grabbed my water glass and downed what was in it. Then she started laughing. "That was hot!"

Lars walked over. We did our usual, *"LAAAARRRSS"* chant.

He said something to Astrid in Swedish and they both cracked up.

"What'd he say?" Zoe asked.

"That's for me to know and for you to find out!" Astrid said, smiling. "How do you girls say it? 'Game on?'"

We all laughed again. "Yep," Nina said. "Game on."

CHAPTER 5

It was clear to us that Lars and Astrid had something up their Swedish sleeves. We were totally on alert for the next few days, checking our beds for short-sheets, making sure there was toilet paper in every stall, inspecting toothpaste for tampering—but nothing happened.

Needless to say, I loved all the pranking fun. It helped me keep my mind off my parents and the possibility that they might be coming to visiting day separately.

And then, Astrid finally struck back.

We were all lying around Nina's bed, playing cards after lights out when we heard a bullfrog noise coming from the other side of the bunk. A giant *ribbit*. Since we were waiting for something weird, we all got up to investigate. A second *ribbit* came from near the door. And we saw Mr. Snuggles, my teddy bear, jumping up and down on the floor. On his own. Mr. Snuggles had suddenly become a frog-teddy bear and had come to life.

Claire screamed the loudest, scariest scream ever, and R^2 ran into our bunk in like a nanosecond.

"What's going on? What's going on?" she panted, sounding totally scared.

Mr. Snuggles ribbeted and jumped, and R^2 backed away from it.

"It's like it's alive," Zoe whispered.

"More like Astrid brought it to life," I said, picking it up. It jumped and ribbeted as I held it. "We just got punked!"

R^2 started cracking up. "She got you! She got you big-time!"

"I don't get it. How'd she do it?" MJ asked.

I grabbed some scissors and opened up Mr. Snuggles's back. Inside was a Jumping Jack Flash toy frog—one that jumped and made noise. It had made the teddy bear look like it was moving and talking.

"Nicely done, Astrid!" I shouted.

Astrid rushed in. "Game over!" she shouted.

We all laughed.

"Sorry, Claire. I didn't mean to completely scare you!" Astrid said.

"That's okay. We deserved it," Claire said.

"How'd you know Mr. Snuggles had some room for secret stuffing?" I asked. We liked to fill up his belly with candy. It was the best way to sneak outlawed treats.

"I was talking to Rachel about pranks. She told me about him," Astrid said.

"For real? How'd you know, R^2?" I couldn't believe that they knew our best bunk secret.

"Your last year's version of Mr. Snuggles leaked candy during inspection one day. I figured you'd do the same thing again this summer."

Astrid started singing some kind of "You know I got you" song. Then she said, "Plus, I have your candy! Ha!"

"Won't you share it with us, since you scared me so badly?" Claire asked, sticking out her lip in a pretend pout.

Astrid laughed. "Okay, we can have a little party right now if it's okay with Rachel."

R^2 said, "Just don't tell anyone—and pass me some Super Novas!"

CHAPTER 6

The next morning, we were all tired from our post-prank bunk party. I had swim during my first activity period. Not looking forward to the splash of cold water, I dragged myself down to the waterfront to practice for the Tri-Camp Games at Camp Laurel Canyon.

As I trudged toward the docks, I saw Angus waving to me. "Hey, mate! You ready to roll?"

I yawned in response.

He laughed. "You're going to have to get on it, because Mac wants to challenge you to a freestyle race. The winner will swim anchor for the relay."

"You're kidding, right?" I replied.

"No, ma'am. She thinks she's got a shot at beating you and asked me to set up a race."

"For real? When?" I asked, definitely starting to wake up a little bit.

"Right now, mate!"

"What? That's not . . . Now? Really?" I couldn't believe it.

"You have nothing to worry about, mate," Angus said. "I'll give you time to warm up and then we'll do it."

I didn't want to complain to Angus, but really? A head-to-head race? With no warning? I mean, everyone knew she couldn't beat me, but I still should have gotten some advance warning. Why was Angus making me do this?

I walked into the boathouse to put my stuff away and grab my goggles. Zeus, the black Lab who was more or less our camp mascot, followed me inside. I bent down to pet him. "I know, Zeusy, I know. It's not fair at all." Zeus gave me a long look. Clearly he agreed with everything I was saying.

That was when the idea hit me. I grabbed my goggles and coaxed Zeus to follow me out to the docks by showing him some of my leftover English muffin from breakfast. He was always wandering around the swimming area, so it was no big deal that he was patrolling the dock with me. I hid the English muffin inside my towel, and I dove into the water. Zeus sat quietly waiting by my lane.

After what seemed like an entire week of camp, Mac and Angus walked over.

"Hey, Em. Thanks so much for doing this," she said with super-fake sweetness.

"Oh, no prob, Mac," I said. "You deserve it." Yeah, right. She deserved what she was about to get. I pulled myself up onto the dock and shook out my arms and legs.

Angus got us set. "Okay, girls. Are you ready?"

We both nodded.

"On your mark, get set, go!" Angus yelled.

When Mac dove in, I flung my English muffin far into my lane, and Zeus dove after it. No hesitation. He was as fast off the block as I was! I collapsed into laughter, sure that Angus would do the same.

Not quite.

Angus jumped into the lake and plucked Zeus out, depositing him on the dock in front of me. Zeus thanked me for the English muffin by shaking himself all over me. Ew.

Mac, in the meantime, finished her race and was looking around to see if she had beaten me. Confused, she finally looked up and saw me on the dock.

"What's going on?" Mac asked. "Did I win?"

"Why don't you tell her, Emily," Angus said, with the kind of quiet voice that's almost worse than yelling. Why was Angus so mad? It was no biggie.

"As a joke, I got Zeus to jump in. I thought it was funny. You know me," I said.

Silence.

"We can race now," I offered. "I was just kidding with the Zeus thing."

"No. We'll just mark Mac down as the winner. Congratulations, Mac. You'll be swimming anchor at Laurel Canyon," Angus said in the same quiet voice.

"What? Angus, that's not fair! I was just playing around!" I exclaimed.

"Angus, I don't want to win like that. I'll race Emily. I don't mind," Mac chimed in.

Was Mac being genuine, or did she just want Angus to think she was nice?

"That's generous of you, mate. But, you'll swim anchor this year. And, you, Emily, will come with me."

I quietly followed Angus to his little office next to the boathouse.

"Angus, why are you so mad?" I finally asked.

"Because you didn't respect your opponent." He paused. "Mac asked for a race straight up. You could have beaten her no problem. But you made fun of her when you sent Zeus into your lane. I can't have that."

"It wasn't like that, Angus. I was tired and you just sprang it on me. I wanted to have a little fun."

"Okay, I get that. It just wasn't funny. It wasn't respectful. You can swim anchor next year. But you lost, fair and square," Angus said, his voice one shade nicer than before. "I don't want to see you messing around like that again. Understood?"

I nodded.

"You can get a swim in now, if you like, or you can go back to main camp." He grabbed his whistle from the hook behind him and went back outside.

Wait, what just happened? I didn't know what to say. And I *always* know what to say.

People have gotten mad when I've done pranks before, but not like this. I still didn't quite get why he was making such a big deal about it. But it was totally embarrassing. I grabbed my stuff from the boathouse and headed back to the bunk. Bumping into Mac would be killer, so I left quickly.

I went into my empty bunk and changed into shorts and a T-shirt. While I was putting on my sneakers, the cabin door opened. Susannah. Next to Mac and Angus, she was the last person I wanted to see.

"Emily! What are you doing here?" she asked. "You're supposed to be at your first activity!"

They didn't report you for cutting activities at camp, but if they did, she would have written me up. For sure.

"I was just down at swimming. Angus let me go early," I said quietly.

She walked toward me. "Are you feeling okay? You never leave swimming early."

My lip started to quiver. "I'm okay," I lied.

"What's wrong, sweetie?" She sat down on my bed and put her hand on my forehead to check for fever. Just like my mom does. "No fever. But I can tell from your face that something's going on."

"I just . . . I just . . . did something stupid and now Angus is mad," I said with a sniffle.

"I'm sure it's nothing that can't be undone. Don't be so hard on yourself, Emily."

She was being so sweet. It actually seemed like she cared. Where was the rules-enforcing counselor we thought was a total pain?

So I spilled. I told her about Zeus and Mac and not being allowed to swim anchor in the race.

"It sounds like you just thought it was going to be funny and Angus saw it differently," she said.

"When you say it like that, it doesn't seem so bad," I said.

"Because it isn't. Do you want me to speak to Angus for you?" she asked.

I shook my head. "No. Definitely not. I can talk for myself. But thank you. You're being so great."

"That's what I'm here for," she said as she brushed the hair out of my face.

"And, Susannah," I paused. "Please don't tell anyone. It's too embarrassing."

She made a motion like she was zipping her lip. "Now go to your next activity. You'll feel better when you're out doing something."

Okay, so she was actually really nice. And really understanding. Who knew?

That was the one bright spot in a lousy day. That afternoon, I got an email from my dad.

Em! I'm so glad that you saw Zac and that you guys had a great time together. Tubing sounds awesome! Can we do that when I come up this year? It's not set in stone, but I'm thinking about coming up a few days before visiting day because I may have to attend a firm retreat that weekend. I know it's not what we planned, but it looks like the firm's two biggest partners are coming in from California. If that happens, they'll want me there. Mom is happy to hold down the fort and visit you on the actual day.

Did he think that Zac and I were stupid? If they weren't coming to visiting day together, it meant that things had gotten worse since we were gone. When we got home, I knew they were going to tell us that they were splitting up. All the more reason to enjoy every minute of camp. But, after my Zeus prank backfired and with Angus mad at me, and Mac swimming anchor, there wasn't a lot to look forward to.

CHAPTER 7

My bunkmates must have realized that something was up with me because I was actually kind of quiet for once. It was just hard to act like my regular self.

Shortly after our afternoon conversation, Susannah, unfortunately, started acting like old, grouchy, follow-the-rules Susannah again. Next day, during our forced rest hour, she banged into the bunk and reamed us for getting a 5.5 in bunk inspection. "You girls are one-tenth of a point away from officially being called pigs."

"Wait, a 5.4 means you're a pig?" MJ asked.

I had to laugh. Susannah shot me a look.

"Look at this bunk! You guys leave your clothes everywhere and then just hide them for inspection."

"We aren't the neatest," Nina said. "But no one's ever called me a pig before."

I could tell that the rest of the girls were starting to get mad. Especially Claire, who's as neat as they come.

"What's the big deal, anyway?" Nina asked. "A perfect score for inspection is 6.0. We're not that far off."

"And anyway, Susannah, only the little kids are obsessed with inspection. Nobody our age really cares," I said.

"Well, I want the bunk completely spotless by tomorrow. You girls need to be considerate about how you keep our cabin." She stormed out the door.

We all looked at one another. I didn't get it. How was Susannah so nice and caring one minute, and then a total sourpuss the next? Was she that moody? Or was she going through a hard time like me?

"Time to prank Ms. Grouch," Nina said.

"Yes, it is," MJ agreed. "Especially since our water balloons have finally arrived." She held out the bag of balloons for all of us to see.

After what happened with Angus and Zeus, I wasn't ready for another person to be mad at me for a prank, and I was surprised to find myself hoping they would change their minds. "Maybe we should give her a week or so to cool off," I suggested.

"She needs to lighten up," Claire said. "And a little fun is good for camp bonding."

"She's really not that bad," I said. "And *she* won't think it's funny."

"But it *would* be funny, wouldn't it?" Zoe said.

"And it would be harmless. Almost as lame as short-sheeting her bed. You said so yourself," MJ added.

"Didn't you just see how crazy she went about extra dust in our pigsty," I argued.

"You're not acting like yourself," Nina said. "You're usually our leader."

"I just wanna know what the point is," I asked. "Getting her mad?"

"No, the point is to have fun! We had fun with Astrid. Let's have fun with Susannah now," Claire said.

We were going to put the water balloon under her pillow. How much trouble could that cause?

But I was still on the fence about doing it. I was worried that Susannah would automatically assume it was my fault, and then she'd regret being nice. Plus, she might tell Angus, and I might not get to swim in the meet at all. But after her pigsty rant, the others were set on pranking her that very night.

That evening's activity was a campfire. Mon Mon's campfires were always really fun. We would toast marshmallows and make s'mores. Then one of the

camp groups would usually give a presentation on the meaning of a word like *truth* or *spirit*.

We all sat on log benches around the fire. I felt super-cozy . . . until Mac plopped down next to me. I hadn't talked to her since the morning's Zeus race, and I didn't want to start now.

It was weird though; I had figured that she would tell everyone at camp—including the chipmunks, squirrels and bats—that she was going to swim anchor in the Tri-Camps. But no one had said anything to me.

"Move over, Emily. I think Bick and Elise want to sit on the end of the bench," she said, smushing me.

I was still waiting for her to mention the race. But . . . nothing.

Then finally, she opened her mouth. *Here it comes*, I thought.

"I think Lars and Astrid are going to talk about Swedish campfires tonight," she said.

That was it? Nothing about anything? Was it Backward Day again? Mac was being nice, and I didn't want to pull a prank. Things were definitely backward.

"Oh yeah. They used to have big bonfires in their town," I said, suspicious that she was going to pounce. And then . . . nothing.

"Let me move over this way to give you some more room," she said.

She was even desmushing. Something had to be up.

CHAPTER 8

After the campfire, we went back to our bunk to set up our Susannah prank. Our plan was simple. Take one of the water balloons, fill it, put it under Susannah's pillow, and then wait. Susannah had the evening off, so we didn't know when she'd come in. We figured that if we fell asleep, we'd be woken up by her screaming.

Astrid came in before Susannah, got ready for bed, then climbed into the top bunk and went to sleep. I was relieved that Astrid would be there when the prank went down. She could stop Susannah from going nuts.

I dozed off sometime after Astrid came in, but I was jolted awake by a noise and then a loud scream. Since we didn't have electricity in the bunk, Susannah couldn't turn on the light to see what had happened. But we were all awake after she shrieked.

Astrid hopped down from the top bunk and asked, "What's going on? Is everyone okay?"

"You tell me," Susannah said.

"Huh?" Astrid replied.

"My head is soaking wet," Susannah said.

A giggle came from across the room, probably from Zoe. (She was always giggling about something.) But then we all started laughing.

"*Oooooh*, so you got punked, huh?" Astrid said innocently.

"Pranked, Astrid," Susannah growled. "You girls think this is funny?"

We were all full-scale laughing.

"You won't think it's so funny when I tell Aunt Alice and you get punished!" she yelled.

"Calm down, Susannah. What actually happened?" Astrid asked.

"I don't know, ask them!" Susannah was steaming.

"Girls?" Astrid said.

Silence.

"My head is totally wet. They put something on my pillow!" Susannah shouted.

"Girls?" Astrid said again, a bit firmer this time.

"Water balloon," I said. "It's nothing harmful or permanent, Astrid."

"Well, you destroyed my pillow. And maybe even the mattress," Susannah said, madder than we could have imagined.

Nina flashed her flashlight at Susannah's bed.

"We can help you clean up. Right, girls?" Astrid said.

"Sure," Nina said, hopping out of bed.

"I can't believe that you would do this. Especially you, Emily. After your latest prank? After everything that happened with Zeus and Angus? I'm going straight to Aunt Alice!" She stormed out, slamming the door behind her.

I pulled the covers over my head. She was going to get me in serious trouble. And she had just told everyone something I told her not to.

"What happened with Angus and Zeus, Emily?" Claire asked.

I pulled myself up. "It was nothing," I said. I really didn't want to get into it.

Nina shined her flashlight on me. "Tell us, Em."

"Do you think she could get us kicked out of camp?" I asked quietly. The thought of it was making me feel worse and worse.

"No!" MJ said. "She's just overreacting. I'm sure that Aunt Alice will think this is funny!"

"For real. I can't get kicked out of camp," I said even more quietly. I sniffed loudly, trying to keep the tears from coming. The thought of being sent home . . .

Nina walked over to my bed and put her arm around my shoulders. "What's going on, Emily? You've never been worried about anything before."

Nina was so sweet, it just killed me—and I finally let my tears fall. I don't think anyone at camp had ever seen me cry before. The other girls gathered around my bed and Astrid walked over.

"Tell us, Em. It can't be that bad," Claire said.

"It is . . ." I said through my tears. "I can't get kicked out. I can't go home." I sniffed.

Astrid moved closer. "No one is going to send you home, Emily. What's on your mind, *sotnos*?"

Somehow that made me laugh. "What's a *sotnos*?" I asked, still sniffling and leaking.

"It is like honey or sweetheart," Astrid explained.

"I think that will be my new nickname for you, Emily. You will be Sotnos."

I laughed again. Then I blew my nose, controlling my sniffling a little bit.

"My parents. They're . . . well, my family is," I stopped. Everyone was crowded around, looking at me. "Things have been really rough at home this year. Zac and I think that our parents are going to break up."

They were all surprised. "Em, I'm so sorry. That has to be awful," Claire said immediately.

I nodded. "They've been fighting all year. I just didn't want to tell anyone. Maybe I just wanted to pretend that it wasn't happening and that everything was the same."

"Oh, Em. This can be your safe place," Nina said, squeezing my arm.

I nodded. "That's why I can't get sent home."

"Sotnos," Astrid said, and I couldn't help but smile. "You don't need to worry. You did a teeny little prank on

Susannah. No one will care. Aunt Alice won't care. You're not going anywhere."

"But I also kind of did something the other day at the waterfront," I said. Everyone was silent. I think they were all afraid to ask.

"Was it what Susannah was talking about as she left?" Zoe finally asked.

I nodded.

"It couldn't have been that bad if she didn't narc on you," MJ replied.

"I didn't think it was," I said. "But Angus got so mad. Basically, I had Zeus jump in to take my place in a race against Mac."

Everyone laughed. "No way!" Claire exclaimed.

"That must have been hil-ar-i-ous," Nina chimed in.

"Did he win?" MJ asked, and Zoe giggled.

I shook my head no. "Angus was super-mad at me. He told me not to do anything like that again."

"So you're afraid that Susannah will say something to Aunt Alice and get you into double trouble?" MJ asked.

"I guess," I admitted.

"We will fix this, Sotnos," Astrid said. "Don't worry. All of this will be settled quickly." She patted my back. "Now, Emily, wash your face, and you'll all help me fix Susannah's bed," Astrid said.

As I washed up in the bathroom, I realized that I had just spilled my big secret. Now everyone knew that I wasn't as tough as I seemed. It was sort of scary. But more than anything, I was relieved.

Claire walked over and started braiding my hair while I was at the sink. "You okay, Sotnos? You know I'm here for you if you need to talk."

"Thanks, Clairey," I said.

Sniffling done, we fixed Susannah's bed. We changed her sheets and put her wet pillow on a chair to dry. I donated my extra pillow to the cause, and we put a fresh pillowcase on it. Then all there was left to do was wait to see what would happen when Susannah came back.

"Maybe you girls should try to get some sleep," Astrid said.

"Somehow, I don't think that's going to happen," Zoe replied.

"Well, then, let's play that game that you girls like . . . two truths and an untruth?" Astrid said.

"Two truths and a lie," MJ said.

"I'll go first," Zoe volunteered. "I've played cricket at school. I've met the Queen of England. I went bungee jumping with my dad."

"We know you've met the queen, Ms. Fancy-Pants," I said.

Zoe laughed.

"You'd never go bungee jumping, would you, Zoe?" Claire asked.

Just as Zoe was about to answer, Susannah walked in. She came straight over to MJ's bed, where we were all sitting.

"Listen, girls," she said quietly. "I think I overreacted. I know you thought it was funny. And maybe if I had been in a better mood, I would have thought it was funny too. I've calmed down now. And anyway, it's no biggie."

"We didn't do it to be mean," Nina said. "It's camp, you know?"

"I know. I know." Susannah paused. "You guys are great. I love being your counselor. I had a long talk with Aunt Alice, and I feel much better. I think maybe I've been being too rules-y."

"Maybe?" I said. Now that the truth was out, I was back to saying everything that popped into my mind.

"Aunt Alice reminded me what camp is all about. So . . . on that note, be prepared for my revenge!" Susannah exclaimed.

"Not this again," Nina said.

Susannah grabbed a pillow and started a pillow fight. I couldn't believe that the prank did what it was supposed to: get Susannah to relax and lighten up!

Once things calmed down and everyone went back to bed, I got up and found Susannah brushing her teeth.

"I just wanted to say I'm sorry that we upset you." I paused.

"I'm sorry I spilled your secret," Susannah said, sheepishly. "It just slipped out by accident."

"It's okay. You were mad. I told the girls everything. Also . . ." I paused. "I hadn't told anyone before tonight, but camp is really important to me because life at home hasn't been so good."

"I think I know what you are saying, and I'm sorry that you've had to deal with that." Susannah's words were making me start to tear up, but somehow, I was okay with that. "Thank you for trusting me, Emily,"

Susannah added. "Let me know if there is anything I can do."

"I will," I said, and even though I'm not the most huggy person, I gave her a huge one and went to bed. I fell asleep dreaming of more pranks and swim meets, happy that I was a Mon Mon camper.

CHAPTER 9

Two days later was our Tri-Camp swim meet at Camp Laurel Canyon. Since Angus had wigged out at me, I had been down to the waterfront and practiced, but we hadn't been exactly friendly. I mostly avoided him, and was very businesslike whenever I had to talk to him. I didn't know if he heard about what happened with Susannah and the prank, or even if he heard about my parents. He didn't say anything, so I didn't either.

I just wanted to swim in the meet and make sure that we won. If it meant that I led off or swam second or third, it didn't matter.

The three camps participating in the swim meet were us, Laurel Canyon, and Pine Meadow. The freestyle relay race was the last of the day because it was the most important.

I hopped in the van to go to the meet and sat down next to Aubrey, another Blue Jay and relay team member. Mac walked down the aisle and sat right behind us.

"You guys ready for the race?" she asked.

"I'm in the zone," Aubrey said.

"Yeah, me too," I replied.

"I'm so excited!" Mac said.

"Okay, we get it. You're swimming anchor. You don't have to rub it in," I said.

"O-kay," she said slowly. "Did I even say anything about swimming anchor? You just jumped on me for absolutely no reason!"

"You know you were thinking it. That's why 'you're so excited,'" I snapped.

"I never even wanted to swim the anchor leg," Mac said, raising her voice.

"That's such a lie," I shouted. "If you didn't want to anchor the race, then why did you challenge me to a race?"

"Okay, I did hope I could swim anchor," she admitted. "But that was before I saw you swim this year. I know you're faster, Emily. I only challenged you because Angus asked me to! You've definitely made me wish I hadn't!"

"What? Why would Angus ask you to do that?" I asked.

"Ask him!" she yelled.

I didn't know what to say. The rest of the van was totally silent because we were shouting. None of this made sense. Backward Day part three.

CHAPTER 10

When we arrived at Laurel, I went looking for Angus. He had gotten there early to help set up the swimming lanes, go over the rules, and stuff like that. I found him on the docks and marched over.

"You guys are here already. Great. Why don't you go into the boathouse over there and get changed, Emily," Angus said when he saw me.

"Angus! Mac said that she never wanted to swim the anchor leg of the race and that it was your idea for her to challenge me. Is that true?" I asked.

"Yes, it was, mate!" he said. "That took you a while to find out!"

"What? Why would you do that?" I was beyond surprised.

"Didn't want you to phone it in. I wanted to make sure you had some competition." He paused and smiled at me. "And I know that nothing motivates you like Mac."

"So you told her to talk it up? To say that she was better than me?"

He nodded. "And your prank? With Zeus?" he said.

"Yeah?"

"It was actually a pretty good one. I dove in after Zeus, because I didn't want you to see me laugh," he said with a grin.

"You tortured me!" I exclaimed. "Totally not nice, Angus!"

"But you're ready to swim aren't you, Emily?" he asked.

"I would have been ready! I suppose you think I'll go even faster now because I'm hating on you!" I said.

"Here's to that!" he said, raising his whistle as if it was a glass. "Now go win the race, mate!"

I was furious. He had made me so mad. Totally worked up about the whole thing. Is this what it's like to be on the other end of a prank? It would serve him right if I swam the slowest laps in the history of the Tri-Camp. But I wanted to win too much.

I found Mac on the docks. "Listen," I said. "Apologizing isn't easy for me. But I know I was a brat, and I'm sorry. We've definitely had our problems at camp over the years, but this time it's on me."

Her eyes got big. Probably she was in shock that I said I was sorry. "It's okay, Emily. I didn't mean to be in your face." She paused. "You can take the anchor leg. I know it means a lot to you."

"No, Mac. But thanks. You won the race and you deserve to swim anchor. Angus even said so," I said.

"But, I'm not as fast as you. I know it," she replied.

"You'll be great," I said. "And we'll make sure you get a big lead."

She laughed. "*Big* big. Like huge."

"Let's go find the rest of the team and win the trophy," I said.

And that's what we did. We set the new Tri-Camp record for the freestyle relay. I have to admit that Mac swam the race of her life.

On the van ride home, wet and happy, I clutched the first-place trophy, ready to show it to Mom or Dad or both on visiting day.

ABOUT THE AUTHOR

Wendy L. Brandes, an attorney, is quite familiar with the excitement, fun, adventure, trials, and tribulations of summer camp. Initially a reluctant camper, she attended summer camp in the Adirondacks for four years and sent both her son and her daughter to camp in Maine. A published legal writer, Wendy notes that she has had far more fun writing this summer camp series and reliving her days as a camper. She lives in Manhattan with her husband, her children and her dog, Louie, a black lab.

ABOUT THE ILLUSTRATOR

Eleonora Lorenzet lives and works in Osnago, a small village in northern Italy. After studying foreign languages in high school with the hopes of traveling the world, she attended the School of Comics of Milan. Eleonora has always wanted to be an artist, but if she wasn't an illustrator, she says she'd be a rock star. Or a witch. Or a character from the manga series *Sailor Moon*.

GLOSSARY

annoy (uh-NOI)—to make someone lose patience or feel angry

counselor (KOUN-suh-lur)—someone trained to help with problems or give advice

DNA (dee-en-AY)—the molecule that carries the genetic code that gives living things their special characteristics

enthusiasm (en-THOO-zee-az-uhm)—great excitement or interest

motivate (MOH-tuh-vate)—to encourage someone to do something

narc (NARK)—slang for telling someone in authority that someone else is doing something wrong

obnoxious (uhb-NOK-shuhss)—very unpleasant, annoying, or offensive

orthodontist (or-thuh-DON-tist)—a dentist who straightens uneven teeth

poison ivy (POI-zuhn EYE-vee)—a shrub or climbing vine with clusters of three shiny, green leaves; poison ivy causes an itchy rash on most people who touch it

sarcastic (sar-KASS-tik)—a person who uses bitter or mocking words that are meant to hurt or make fun of someone or something

stranded (STRAND-ehd)—to leave in a strange or unpleasant place, especially without any way to depart

unison (YOO-nuh-suhn)—people that say, sing, or do something together

GATHER 'ROUND THE CAMPFIRE

1. What were some of the ways the campers celebrated Backward Day? What other ideas can you come up with for this mixed-up day?

2. In chapter 9, Emily loses her temper with Mac on the bus. What did you think of how Emily handled the conversation? How could she have handled it differently? How would that have changed the story?

3. Do you think Susannah is a bad counselor? Use examples from the text to support your answer.

GRAB A PEN AND PAPER

1. Emily loves to swim, but she doesn't really like doing the butterfly stroke. Make a list of things you do and do not like about your favorite sport.

2. Write a scene that takes place while the group of friends is tubing on Brother–Sister Day. Does everyone get along?

3. Pretend you are Emily. Write a letter to Mac explaining why you were annoyed with her and apologize for being short–tempered. Use examples from the text.

CHECK OUT MORE ADVENTURES!

≫—SUMMER CAMP→

MJ'S CAMP CRISIS

CAMP MON MON LAKE

BY WENDY L. BRANDES

≫—SUMMER CAMP→

EMILY'S PRANKING PROBLEM

BY WENDY L. BRANDES

≫—SUMMER CAMP→

CLAIRE'S CURSED CAMPING TRIP

BY WENDY L. BRANDES

≫—SUMMER CAMP→

NINA'S NOT BOY CRAZY! (SHE JUST LIKES BOYS)

BY WENDY L. BRANDES